# Plenty to Watch

*Also by Mitsu and Taro Yashima*

MOMO'S KITTEN

*by Taro Yashima*

THE VILLAGE TREE
CROW BOY
UMBRELLA
YOUNGEST ONE
SEASHORE STORY

To our daughter Momo

*Grateful acknowledgment is made
to Dr. and Mrs. John Vincent, Mr. Irving Fineman,
and Mrs. Anne Walters, whose encouragement
at the Huntington Hartford Foundation
made this book possible.*

Copyright 1954 by Mitsu and Taro Yashima. All rights reserved. First published in 1954
by The Viking Press, Inc., 625 Madison Avenue, New York, N.Y. 10022. Published simul-
taneously in Canada by The Macmillan Company of Canada Limited. Library of Congress
catalog card number: 54–12294. Seventh printing October 1969. Printed in U.S.A.
Pic Bk

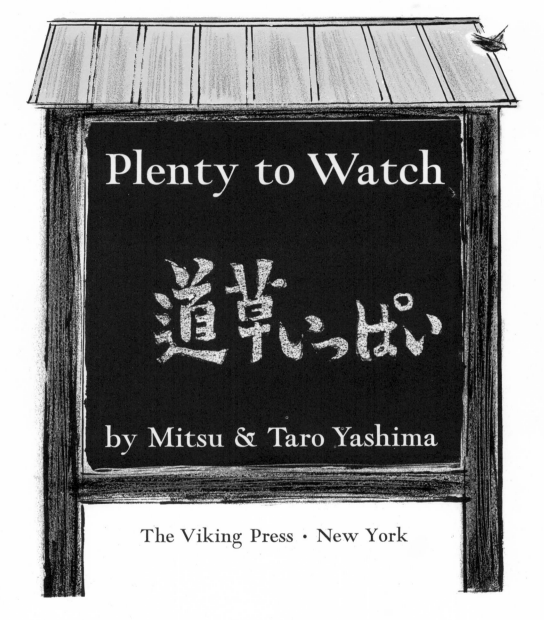

# Plenty to Watch

道草いっぱい

by Mitsu & Taro Yashima

The Viking Press · New York

This is the village school we went to a long time ago in Japan, when we were little like you.

We learned many things there every day.

But after lessons we hurried out of school because

on our way home there was so much to watch.

Right on the way to the center of the village there lived a
barrel maker. He made things like water buckets, rice containers,
washtubs, and pickle barrels. The sound "tanko, tanko, tanko"
always came from his shop, so we called him Mr. Tanko.

When he made the bands to fasten around the outside of the
barrels the sliced bamboo strips crawled and jumped like snakes.

A little farther on there was a dye house. Here an old man dyed yarns and cloth in smelly vats sunk in the ground. He made the colors himself.

People called him Mr. Blue because his arms were blue even when he wasn't working.

The dyed yarns and the cloth were beautiful when they got dry.

Right in the center of the village was a sweets shop filled with the exciting smell of sugar and flour.

Inside the store a pale-skinned man from a faraway town always sat baking ten, twenty, a hundred turtle-shaped cakes stuffed with tasty bean jam.

The baker's wife made the candy. It was fun to watch a ball of sweet-potato taffy grow into many skinny ropes from a fat rope, and then into a thousand pieces of candy.

Across from the sweets shop there was the shop where an old
master and his apprentices made straw mattresses. Mattresses
were made of thickly woven and pressed straw covered with
clean reed mats. In every house everybody sits, eats, and sleeps
on these mattresses.

When the master trimmed the edge of the straw mattress his wide knife made strange sounds like "zagut, zagut, zagut."

The old master's elbow skin was really thick, like the skin on the soles of his feet, because for many long years he had been using his elbow to hold the reed mats tightly to the pressed straw as he sewed them together.

Next door to the mattress maker was the lantern man's shop.
He made umbrellas and lanterns, using oiled papers. We thought
his bald head looked just like one of his own lanterns.

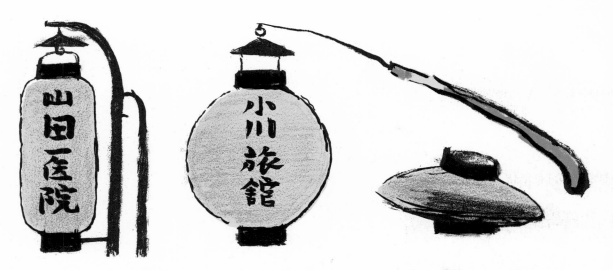

Sometimes we knew who had ordered the lanterns because he painted the family's name on them with black paint.

Many umbrellas, waiting to dry in the backyard, looked like the mushrooms in a storybook.

The door to the studio of the sign painter was usually closed,
but we never missed peeking in when it was open.

We all envied the sign painter because his pictures looked so real and he owned so many brushes.

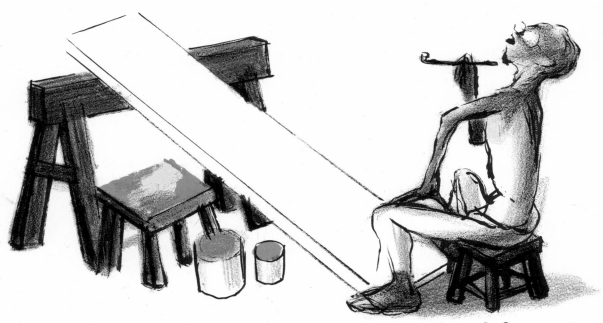

We thought he must be the best painter in the whole country because he was alive, and all the great ones we read about in books were not living.

Toward the end of the village center there was a shop where
the red-cheeked mother of many children made bean-curd cakes
from steamed beans.

The bean-curd cake we called "tofu" was a wonderful food.
Everybody loved to eat it, raw or cooked.

We felt sorry when we saw a lonely man or woman without
any family, taking home only one cake of "tofu."

At the very end of the village center there was a deaf-mute always working hard repairing wooden clogs. A deaf-mute is a person who is not able to hear or speak.

Next door a one-legged man worked a rice-pounding machine all day long. Rice is not ready to boil and eat until the husks are taken off by pounding.

Sometimes we took the mountain road home instead of the road
through the village. Things were quite different there.

The first thing we looked for was the camphor factory. Here lumps of pure white camphor were made from camphor wood.

There was an old man who was always chopping the raw camphor logs, which smelled so cool and clean.

The chopped logs had to be steamed to draw out the camphor juice, so there was always a fire burning on the big hearth. In the winter time, with the refreshing smell of camphor all around us, we felt warm and wonderful, crouching up close to it.

Beyond the camphor factory was a mill where fertilizer was made from animal bones. Fertilizer is important to make the rice grow. We wondered and wondered that the water could turn such a big wheel, and that the wheel could work the huge machines in the mill.

The huge machines shook the ground and scared us a bit. But
we never got tired of watching them at their work.

Behind the mill was the place where sugar canes were being crushed to get juice to make sugar. A bullock turned the treadmill of the great sugar press.

When the bullock was not working we thought it was because
he got dizzy turning the treadmill.

Even the crushed sugar canes had some sweet juice left in them.
We were allowed to take some and chew on them.

Where the mountain road met the road through the village was
the blacksmith's shop. The blacksmith's name was Tora. Tora
means tiger.

That was his real name and he was never afraid of putting the
red-hot horseshoe on the horse's hoof.

After the horseshoes were put on, each horse made a funny face
when he started to walk.

Beyond the blacksmith's place was the barbershop, where we
had to go and sit for our haircuts before holidays.

The hair clipper was old and it pulled and hurt. But we did not mind because we could look in the mirror and see a picture of all the outdoors, just like a foreign land.

With our clipped hair we could make many letters on the white apron.

There were no more stores and workshops, but we could go from one farmer's yard through the next. There we could always find something going on.

Tool sharpening

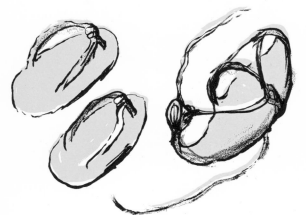

Straw-sandal making

Animal feeding

Firewood chopping

Fence mending

Wagon-wheel greasing

Rice pounding

Bean grinding

Rice winnowing

Rope making

Straw-mat making

Persimmon drying

Radish drying

Working with bamboo

Sometimes when a farmer stopped work to have tea with his family we were invited to join them.

So, when we reached home, almost always it was just before suppertime.

On our way home, as well as in school, we learned many things that helped us grow up.